🌸 A GOLDEN BOOK • NEW YORK

BARBIE and associated trademarks and trade dress are owned by, and used under license from, Mattel, Inc.
Barbie and The Three Musketeers copyright © 2009 Mattel, Inc.
Barbie & The Diamond Castle copyright © 2008 Mattel Inc.
Barbie Mariposa copyright © 2008 Mattel, Inc.
All Rights Reserved.
Published in the United States by Golden Books, an imprint of Random House Children's Books, a division of
Random House, Inc., 1745 Broadway, New York, NY 10019, and in Canada by Random House of Canada
Limited, Toronto. The stories contained in this work were originally published separately by Golden Books in
2008 and 2009. Golden Books, A Golden Book, A Little Golden Book, the G colophon, and the distinctive gold
spine are registered trademarks of Random House, Inc.
www.randomhouse.com/kids
Library of Congress Number: 2009928664
ISBN: 978-0-375-85918-2
PRINTED IN SINGAPORE
10 9 8 7 6 5 4

Long ago, in a small village in France, there lived
a beautiful girl named Corinne. Every day, Corinne
practiced her fencing with her pet kitten, Miette.

"*En garde!*" Corinne cried as she swung her broom
like a sword. She dreamed of one day becoming a
Musketeer—a special protector of the royal family.

Corinne soon set off for Paris with Miette. But once she arrived, Corinne was told that girls could not be Musketeers. She was heartbroken!

Just then, a dog started chasing Miette. Corinne ran
after them. She was in such a rush that she ran right into a
puddle and splashed past a girl named Viveca.

Then Corinne bumped into a girl named Aramina . . .

and knocked over another girl named Renée.

Corinne finally caught Miette near the castle, where she was offered a job as a maid. With nowhere else to go, Corinne accepted.

The other maids were not very happy to meet Corinne—they were the three girls she had splashed, bumped, and knocked over! Luckily, they forgave Corinne, and they all became friends.

Meanwhile, preparations for a masquerade ball were under way. The ball was to be a celebration in honor of Prince Louis, who was going to be crowned king. But the prince's royal advisor, Philippe, had other ideas. Philippe wanted to be king himself, and he was secretly plotting to overthrow the prince.

One day, as Prince Louis walked through the castle's great hall, the ceiling started to collapse! The four girls sprang into action. Corinne used her duster as a sword to smash the falling stones. Viveca used her towel to crack bricks. Aramina kicked rocks. And Renée used her duster to shatter broken glass. Everyone was saved!

Corinne, Viveca, Renée, and Aramina were amazed by each other's skills. And the girls soon discovered that they shared the dream of becoming a Musketeer!

Hélène, an old housekeeper, overheard the girls and told them to follow her. She led them down a long, dark hall to a secret door. Behind it was the Musketeers' old training room!

"Do you think you can be Musketeers?" Hélène asked.
The girls couldn't wait to start their training!

Corinne, Viveca, Aramina, and Renée practiced every day.

"People still believe that girls cannot be Musketeers," said Hélène. "It's up to you to prove them wrong."

One afternoon, the girls heard someone cry for help.

A rope on Prince Louis's hot-air balloon had mysteriously been cut—and he was dangling from it dangerously!

Wasting no time, Corinne swung out the castle window and helped the prince back into his balloon.

"Thank you," Prince Louis said. He had never met a
girl as brave and daring as Corinne. And Corinne had
never met anyone as kind and brilliant as the prince. As
they floated over Paris together, they began to fall in love.

Later that day, Corinne noticed men unloading boxes for the masquerade ball. Inside were real swords!

Corinne tried to warn Philippe and the castle guards that the prince was in danger. But Philippe didn't listen—and he banished Corinne and her friends from the castle forever.

The girls would not let that stop them from protecting Prince Louis!

"All for one and one for all!" they cried, joining hands.

Viveca designed four costumes. Then Aramina taught
everyone how to dance, and Renée sketched a map of
the castle.

"We can do this!" said Corinne.

Corinne, Viveca, Renée, and Aramina disguised themselves in glittering gowns. The guards didn't recognize them as they entered the castle for the masquerade ball.

Prince Louis was amazed by Corinne's beauty and chose her for the first dance. "You look familiar," said the prince. "Do I know you?"

Suddenly, Philippe and his men surrounded the prince with their swords!

But the four friends were ready!
"Prepare for battle!" Corrine shouted.
The girls used their swords, ribbons, fans, and
bow and arrow to stop Philippe's men.

During the commotion, Philippe kidnapped the prince and took him to the castle's rooftop. Luckily, Corinne spotted them and followed.

"You will never be king!" Corinne told Philippe.

Philippe raised his sword, but Corinne quickly defeated him with her fencing skills.

To reward their bravery, King Louis declared that Corinne, Viveca, Renée, and Aramina were Musketeers.

"All for one and one for all!" the four friends cried.

Their adventures together had just begun!

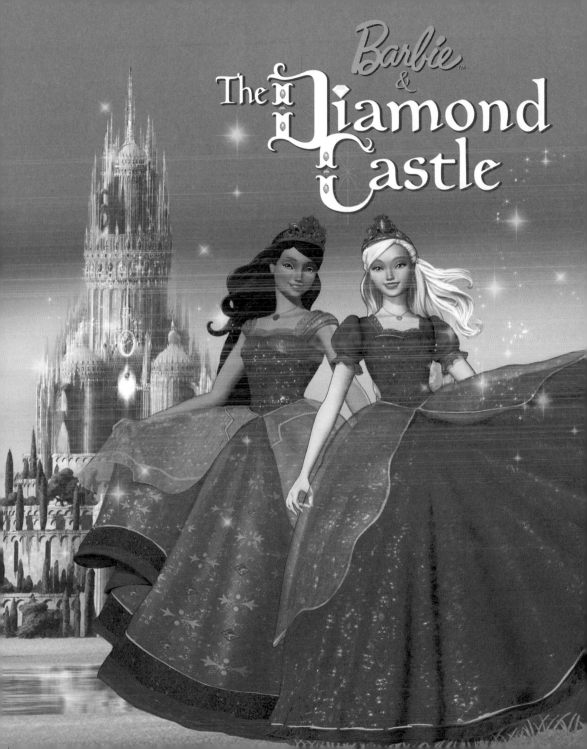

Long ago, there were two best friends who lived together in a humble cottage in the woods. Liana and Alexa didn't have much money or fancy dresses, but they shared everything—especially their love of singing!

One day, the friends found two perfect heart-shaped stones and made them into beautiful necklaces—one for each of them.

"Best friends today, tomorrow, and always!" Liana and Alexa both closed their eyes and made a wish.

They didn't notice that the necklaces began to glow. . . .

Later that day, Liana and Alexa met an old woman near their cottage. The woman was very hungry, so they offered her all the food they had. For their kindness, the woman gave them a small mirror.

Back home, the girls began to sing their favorite song—and were astonished when they heard a third voice join them. It was coming from the mirror!

The two friends discovered that a girl named Melody was hiding inside the mirror. Melody came from a magical place called the Diamond Castle, where the guardians of music, called muses, lived. The Diamond Castle was the birthplace of all music, and every time someone sang a new song, a precious jewel would appear on the sparkling palace.

Melody told the girls about a very selfish muse named Lydia who wanted to rule the entire kingdom. Playing her enchanted flute, Lydia had tried to take over the Diamond Castle. Luckily, the other muses had magically hidden the castle and given Melody the only key to find it.

Lydia had been very angry. She played her flute and
turned the muses to stone. Melody escaped and hid in the
old woman's mirror. And she didn't utter a sound until she
heard the two girls singing.

That was all Lydia's helper, Slyder, needed to find her. He
heard Melody singing with the girls and alerted Lydia.

Alexa and Liana wanted to help Melody return to the
Diamond Castle and rescue the muses. Melody told them
that they had to travel west, toward the Seven Stones.
The girls quickly set off.

Along the way, Alexa and Liana found two lost
puppies, whom they named Lily and Sparkles.

Unfortunately, the girls also ran into a mean troll who wouldn't let them continue their journey unless they could solve his riddle: "What instrument can you hear but not see or touch?"

"Your voice—when you sing," Liana answered correctly.

Furious, the troll disappeared in a puff of smoke! Alexa and Liana quickly went on their way.

Not long after, a dark shadow filled the sky. It was Lydia, riding on Slyder's back!

"Give me the mirror and you can have all this," the evil muse said, offering glittering jewels to Alexa and Liana.

But they wouldn't betray their friend Melody.
Angered, Lydia tried to turn the girls into stone with
her enchanted flute. Fortunately, Alexa and Liana were
protected by their stone necklaces.

The girls and the puppies ran and ran until they reached a beautiful manor on a hilltop. Inside were tables full of food and closets filled with pretty dresses. The manor was everything the girls could ever wish for.

"We can't stay," Liana said. "Melody's in trouble."

But Alexa didn't want to go. She was hungry, tired, and a little afraid.

Sadly, Liana left the manor with Melody and Sparkles.

Alexa couldn't believe that Liana had chosen Melody over her! She tore off her necklace and threw it on the floor.

Just then, Lydia appeared. She had created the manor
as a trap!

"Your spell won't work," Alexa declared.

"Brave words for a girl who no longer wears her
necklace," Lydia said, and played an eerie tune on her flute.

Alexa soon fell under Lydia's spell—and revealed that
Liana and Melody were heading for the Seven Stones.
"After them!" Lydia ordered Slyder.

Slyder quickly found Liana and the mirror and brought them back to Lydia's lair. The evil muse demanded that Melody reveal the location of the Diamond Castle. When Melody refused, Lydia ordered the spellbound Alexa to walk toward a pit of molten lava!

Melody had to save Alexa. "You win, Lydia," she said sadly. "I'll take you to the Diamond Castle."

As Lydia left with Melody, Slyder pushed Liana and Alexa into the bubbling lava pit! Luckily, the girls landed safely on a narrow ledge.

Liana heard barking from above. It was Lily—with Alexa's stone necklace.

"Best friends today, tomorrow, and always!" Liana put the necklace on Alexa, and Alexa slowly opened her eyes and smiled. The spell was broken!

Liana and Alexa soon found Lydia in a misty glade. When the evil muse spotted the girls, she cast a spell on a pond and it became a churning whirlpool. "Now come to me!" Lydia commanded as she played her enchanted flute.

Pretending to be mesmerized, Liana and Alexa walked toward the whirlpool. Then, at the last moment, Liana grabbed the flute from Lydia and threw it into the swirling water.

"No!" Lydia cried. She leapt after her flute and was pulled down into the whirlpool's murky depths.

With Lydia gone, Liana and Alexa used Melody's key
to find the Diamond Castle—the key was a special song!
The girls began to sing, and the Diamond Castle
magically appeared. As they passed through the castle's
jeweled halls, their dresses turned into beautiful gowns and
Melody was set free from the mirror.

Just then, Lydia rode into the castle on Slyder! Melody quickly grabbed the Diamond Castle's enchanted insruments and handed them to Liana and Alexa. The girls started to play and sing in perfect harmony.

"No!" Lydia cried.

The girls' beautiful music turned the evil muse and Slyder into stone!

The beautiful music broke Lydia's evil spell. The muses were saved! For their bravery and kindness, Liana and Alexa were appointed Princesses of Music and invited to live at the Diamond Castle. But instead, they decided to return with the puppies to their humble cottage.

"Best friends today, tomorrow, and always!"

Bibble didn't know what to do. His puffball pal, Dizzle, had invited him for a visit. But Bibble wasn't sure he would fit in with all of Dizzle's friends. So Bibble decided to ask his friend Elina for advice.

"Let me tell you a story about a good friend of mine named Mariposa . . . ," said Elina.

Mariposa lived in a kingdom of beautiful butterfly fairies in a magical place called Flutterfield. But the butterfly fairies didn't like the dark, because that was when the hungry Skeezites came out.

Queen Marabella filled the trees with magical glowing flowers to keep the Skeezites away. As long as Marabella lived, Flutterfield was safe.

But Mariposa was different from all the other fairies. She liked the dark sky because she loved studying the stars. "Look," Mariposa said as she pointed out a constellation to her best friend, Willa. "There's the Archer's bow and arrow."

But Willa was scared of the dark. "We'd better get going before the Skeezites come out," she said.

Mariposa and Willa worked for two sisters
named Rayna and Rayla.

"I have nothing to wear to the ball tonight!" said
Rayna. "Mariposa, have all my gowns befluttered."

"And I need shiny thistleburst for my hair, Willa,"
demanded Rayla. "The prince is going to be at the
ball, and we have to look perfect."

With their arms full of fairy dresses, Mariposa
and Willa hurried to get the two sisters ready for
the ball.

Later that day, Rayna, Rayla, and Willa eagerly arrived at the palace ball. But Mariposa didn't want to go inside, because she didn't think she'd fit in. She decided to stay outside and read a book.

Outside the palace, Mariposa saw Henna, the queen's royal assistant. Henna was very popular and fit in with any crowd.

"Are you coming to the ball?" asked Henna.

"No, I just don't think I'd have much fun," Mariposa explained. "But you wouldn't understand."

"Sometimes I don't feel as if I belong, either," said Henna as she flew toward the palace doors. "But I'll get to where I want to be."

Mariposa thought Henna was a very kind fairy—but Henna had a dark secret! She was plotting to poison the queen and take over Flutterfield!

As Mariposa flew around the palace reading her book, she bumped into Prince Carlos. He didn't like parties, either, and was reading the same book as Mariposa.

The prince was impressed by Mariposa's knowledge of the stars and her interest in faraway places.

Later that night, he asked Mariposa for her help.

"The queen is very sick," said the prince. "Without her, Flutterfield's lights will go out and we will all be in danger. Can you take this map and find the cure?"

Mariposa promised to help, but she wasn't sure she could do it on her own.

When Rayna and Rayla heard about Mariposa's secret mission for the prince, they volunteered to help.

"We will be the ones to save Flutterfield, win the queen's undying gratitude, and impress the prince!" said Rayla.

Mariposa, Rayna, and Rayla quickly set off on their journey. Soon the safety of Flutterfield's lights was far behind them—and Skeezites were everywhere! And to make matters worse, Rayna lost the map!

Mariposa remembered they needed to go east to a place called the Bewilderness. Using her knowledge of the stars, she located the Archer's arrow, which pointed east, and followed it.

In the Bewilderness, they met Zinzie the Meewah.
Zinzie didn't know where the cure was, but she knew two
beautiful mermaids who could help them.

The mermaids agreed to help only if the fairies brought them rare Conkle Shells in return. Mariposa, Rayna, Rayla, and Zinzie dove into the water and soon found the Conkle Shells—but woke the Sea Beast! Luckily, the fairies worked together and quickly escaped the monster.

"Head east and you will find the cure in the Cave of Reflection," the mermaids said as they disappeared with their precious shells.

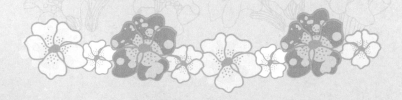

The friends flew for hours and finally reached the
Cave of Reflection. As they entered the cave, they
met a tiny fairy called the Fairy Speck.

"Your journey will end in the star chamber," said
the Fairy Speck. "The cure is hidden there behind a
star. Only one of you may choose the correct star."

Mariposa didn't think she could do it, but
Rayna and Rayla knew she was the bravest and
smartest fairy for the job.

"I know the Archer is a navigator," Mariposa said
as she looked up at a constellation. "His arrow will
point to the correct star." But the arrow was pointing
to one lone star that didn't fit in with the others.
She wondered if that could be the correct star.

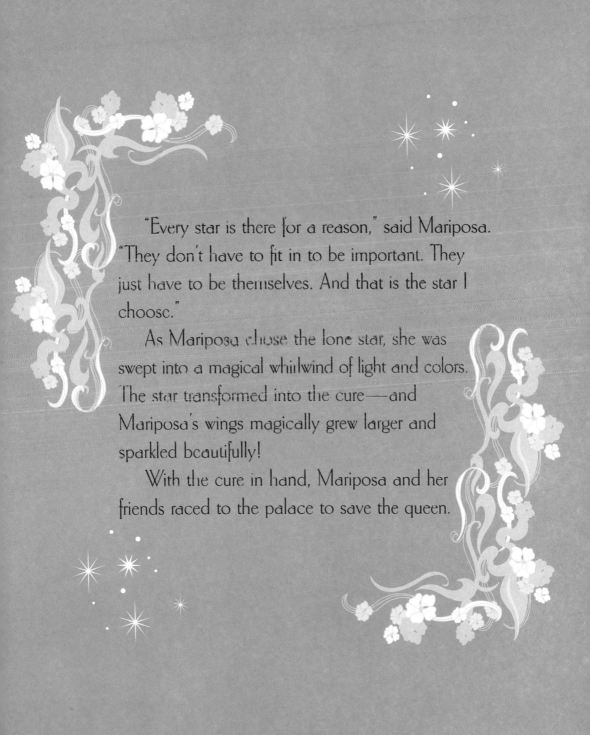

"Every star is there for a reason," said Mariposa. "They don't have to fit in to be important. They just have to be themselves. And that is the star I choose."

As Mariposa chose the lone star, she was swept into a magical whirlwind of light and colors. The star transformed into the cure—and Mariposa's wings magically grew larger and sparkled beautifully!

With the cure in hand, Mariposa and her friends raced to the palace to save the queen.

As the lights slowly went out in Flutterfield,
Henna took control of the kingdom with her horrible
Skeezites. Prince Carlos tried to hold off the
Skeezites, but there were just too many of them.

Mariposa flew quickly through the palace and
discovered Henna in the queen's chambers.

"You've never felt as if you belonged in Marabella's
kingdom," Henna told Mariposa, trying to trick her.
"But you will in mine. Everyone will love you."

"I'm happy with who I am," Mariposa declared
as she flew to the queen's side with the cure. Queen
Marabella awoke and Flutterfield shone brightly.
The Skeezites quickly fled—along with the evil fairy,
Henna. "This isn't over, Flutterfield!" Henna shrieked.
"I'll be back!"

Flutterfield was saved!

Prince Carlos and Queen Marabella were very grateful and gave Mariposa, Rayna, Rayla, and Zinzie beautiful fairy headbands as a reward.

As Mariposa flew away with her fairy friends,
she realized she was special just as she was.

"So you see, Bibble," Elina said, "the most beautiful thing you can be is yourself."

Just then, Dizzle appeared. "Ready to go, Bibble?"

Bibble looked at Elina and smiled. "You bet!" he said. He wasn't afraid of not fitting in anymore. He knew he was special just as he was.